Let's read it!

IT'S A SIGN!

MO WILLEMS'
ELEPHANT & PIGGIE
LIKE READING!

By Jarrett Pumphrey
and Jerome Pumphrey

Sign me up!

An **ELEPHANT & PIGGIE LIKE READING!** Book

Hyperion Books for Children / *New York*

Hi, Two! I am making a sign for my club.

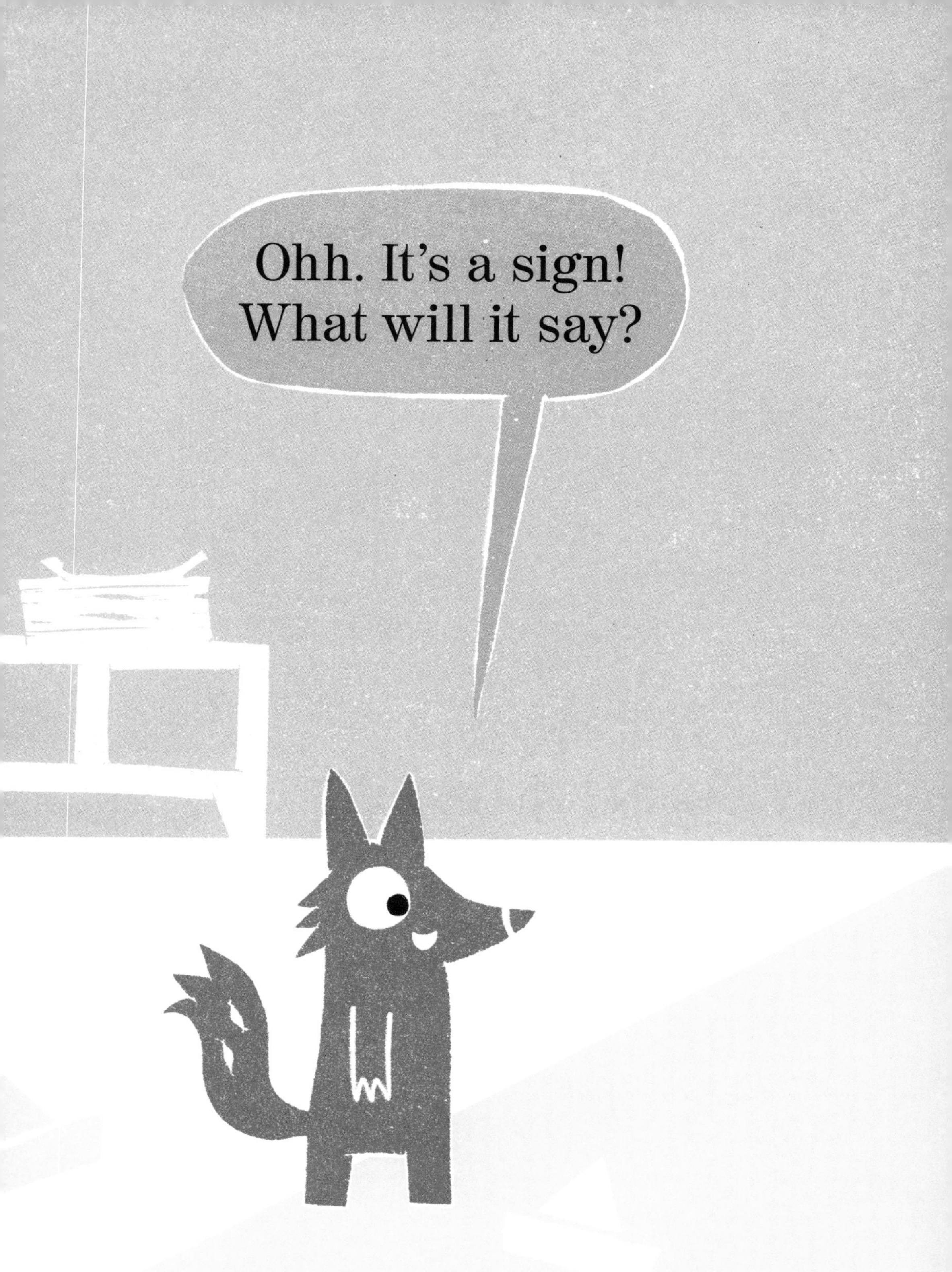
Ohh. It's a sign! What will it say?

I do not know.

I can fold paper hats.

I cannot write.

I know EVERY letter!

You do?

SCRIBBLE

SCRIBBLE

SCRIBBLE

Nice "a," One and Two!

Isn't "a" a word?

It is a letter AND a word. Some words are just one letter long.

Cool! I can write longer words.

You can write longer words?

Will you join our new club?

Yes. Clubs are where it's AT!

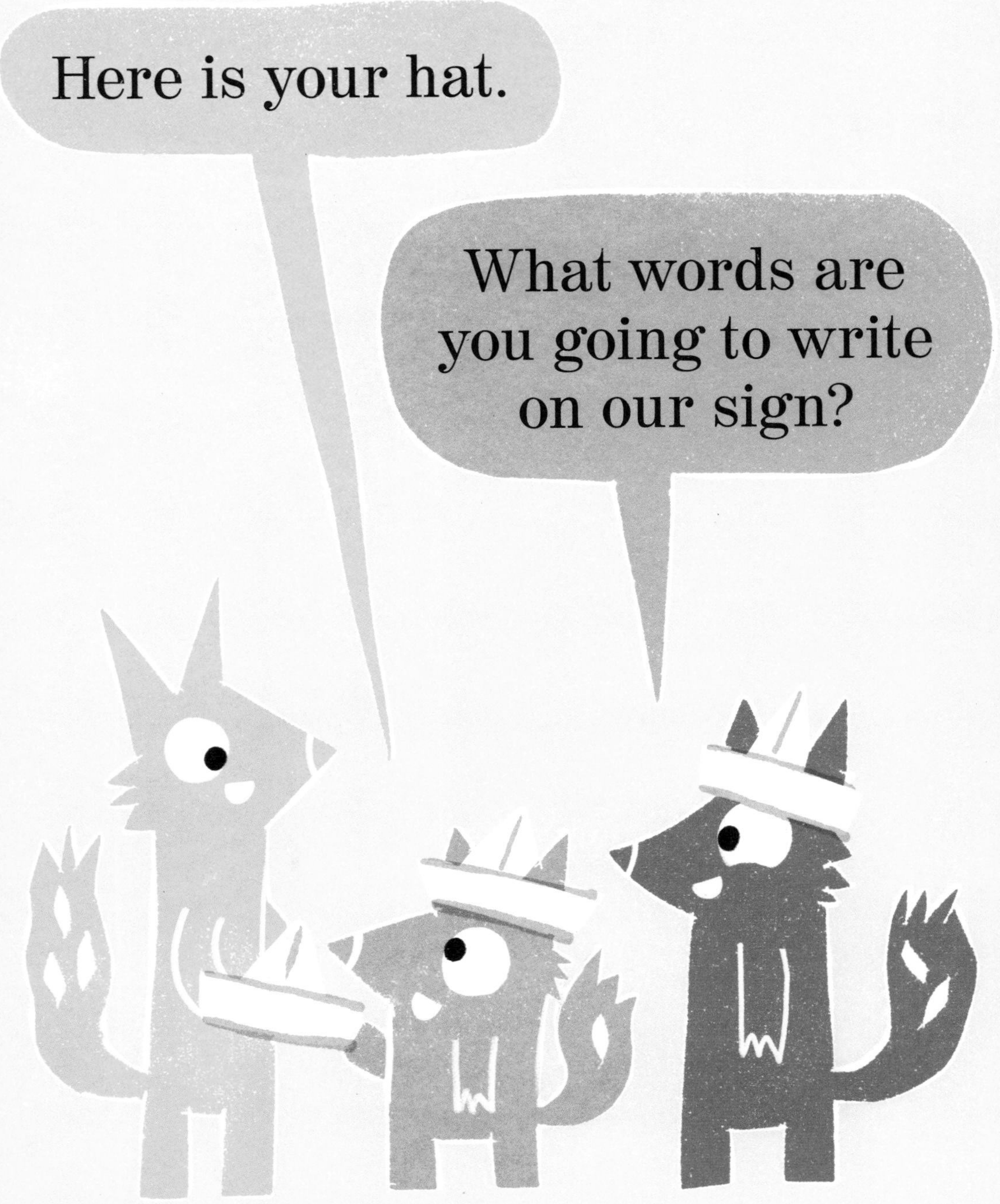
Here is your hat.
What words are you going to write on our sign?

SCRIBBLE

SCRIBBLE

SCRIBBLE

Ta-da!

What does it say?

My name: "KAT"!

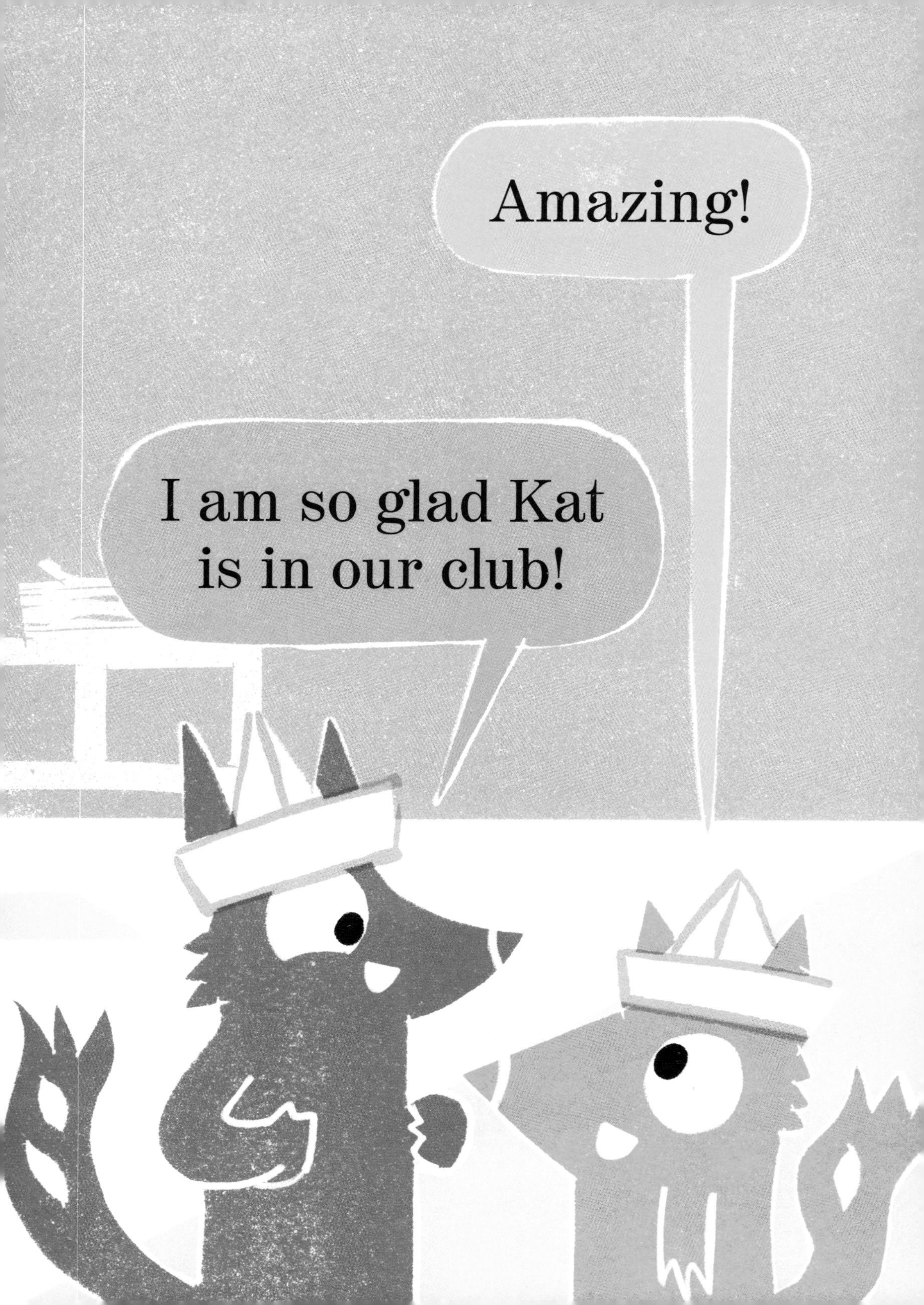
Amazing!
I am so glad Kat is in our club!

And I can write
lots of other words.

SCRIBBLE

SCRIBBLE

SCRIBBLE

Like "BAT."

SCRIBBLE

SCRIBBLE

SCRIBBLE

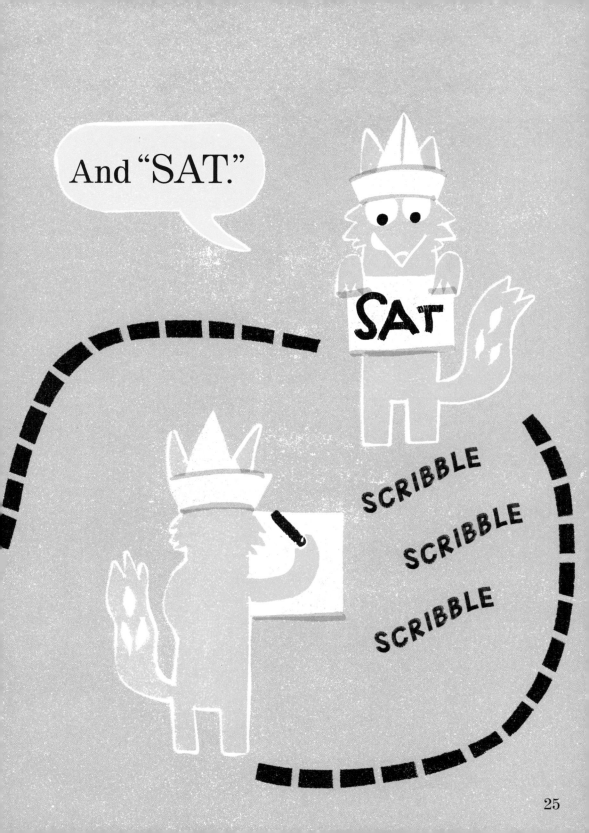

And "MAT."

MAT

SCRIBBLE

SCRIBBLE

SCRIBBLE

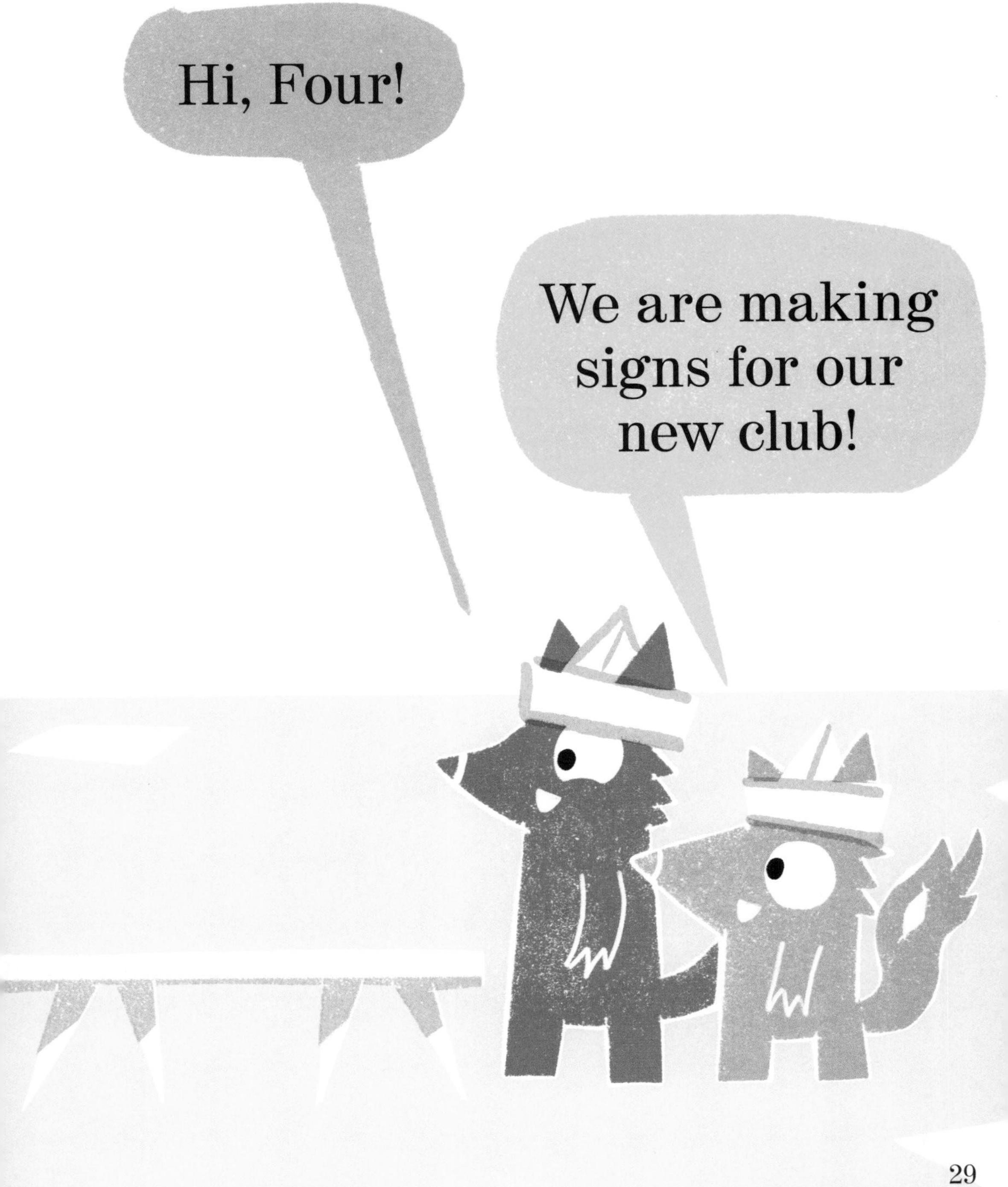
Hi, Four!
We are making signs for our new club!

31

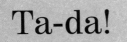

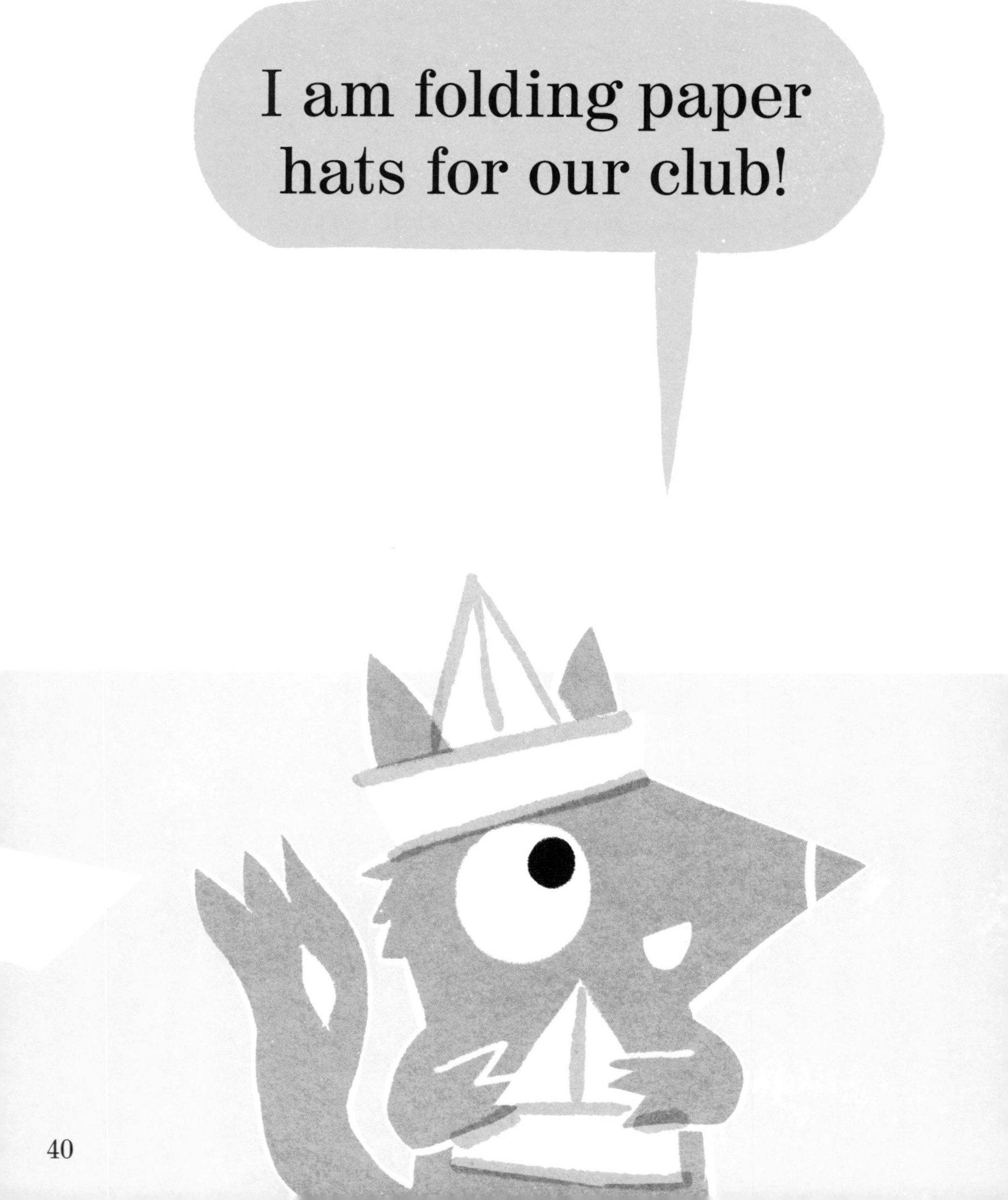
I am folding paper hats for our club!

41

I am writing longer words for our club!

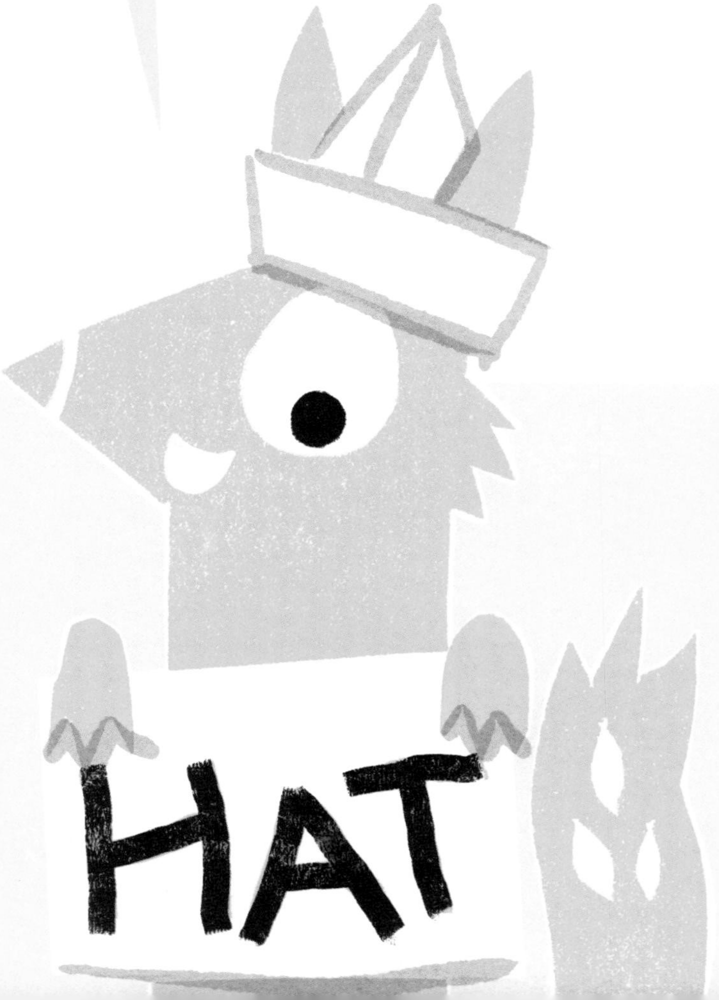

44

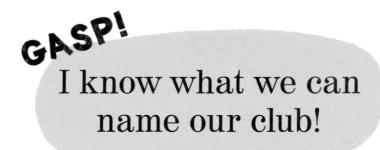

GASP!

I know what we can name our club!

"THE PAPER-FOLDING-LETTER-WRITING-WORD-FORMING-SIGN-MAKING CLUB"!
a

49

Or do you think
that name is taken?

SCRIBBLE

SCRIBBLE

SCRIBBLE

For Jason and Eric, the One and Four
of our very first club.

And special thanks to Mo for welcoming us to the Making-Books-
Elephant-And-Piggie-Like-Reading-So-Much-That-They-Share-Them-
With-All-Of-Their-Friends Club.

First Edition, May 2022 • 1 3 5 7 9 10 8 6 4 2 • FAC-020093-22084 • Printed in the United States of America

This book is set in Century 725/Monotype; Grilled Cheese BTN/Fontbros, with hand-lettering by Jarrett and
Jerome Pumphrey.

The illustrations in this book were created with hand-cut foam stamps and colored digitally.
Library of Congress Cataloging-in-Publication Data
Names: Pumphrey, Jarrett, author. • Pumphrey, Jerome, illustrator. • Willems, Mo, illustrator.
Title: It's a sign! : an Elephant & Piggie like reading! book / by Jarrett Pumphrey and Jerome
Pumphrey, Mo Willems.
Description: First edition. • New York : Hyperion Books for Children, 2022.
  • Series: Elephant & Piggie like reading! • Audience: Ages 4–8 •
  Audience: Grades 1–3 • Summary: One, Two, Kat, and Four want to form a club so
together they figure out how to make a sign saying what their club should be called.
Identifiers: LCCN 2021037391 • ISBN 9781368075848 (hardback) • Subjects: CYAC:
Cooperativeness—Fiction. • Friendship—Fiction. • Clubs—Fiction. •
Writing—Fiction. • Problem solving—Fiction. • Classification:
LCC PZ7.P97328 It 2022 • DDC [E]—dc23 • LC record available at
https://lccn.loc.gov/2021037391

Reinforced binding
Visit hyperionbooksforchildren.com
and pigeonpresents.com